Guion the Lion
A Colorful World

Written by Rebecca Wilson Macsovits
Illustrated by Joseba Morales

Inspire on Purpose Publishing
Irving, Texas

Guion the Lion
A Colorful World

Copyright © 2014 Rebecca Wilson Macsovits

All rights reserved, including the right of reproduction in whole or in part in any form without prior written permission, except in the case of brief quotations embodied in critical reviews and certain other noncommercial uses permitted by copyright law.

Inspire On Purpose Publishing
Irving, Texas
(888) 403-2727
http://inspireonpurpose.com

The Platform Publisher™
Printed in the United States of America

Library of Congress Control Number: 2014953155
ISBN 13: 978-1-941782-02-6

To my Guion - thank you for brightening
my world every day.

"Look out, world. Here I come!" shouted Guion the Lion as he sprinted across the savannah.

When this colorful ball of fur stopped to catch his breath, he found himself in a strange new land.

"How odd!" Guion said. "This place needs some pizzazz!"

The eager little lion grabbed his paints from his pack and brushed the rocks.

Instantly, the colors vanished.

"Hmm! What happened?" he thought, looking at his own bright self.

"Wait a minute! Maybe the color got turned off – like a light switch. I just need to flip it back on. But where could it be?"

The determined lion set out to brighten this gray place.

"Not behind here, either."

Guion was running out of places to search!

"Oops!" Guion tripped over Ostrich, her bottom squiggling in the air. "That's one crazy dance!"

"My head's stuck!" Ostrich cried.

"Well, that's no fun." Guion pulled as he counted, "One, two, threee!"

Out came Ostrich's head with a giant "POP!"

"Whew! Thanks!" Smoothing her feathers, Ostrich added, "You're a life saver. No one else even stopped!"

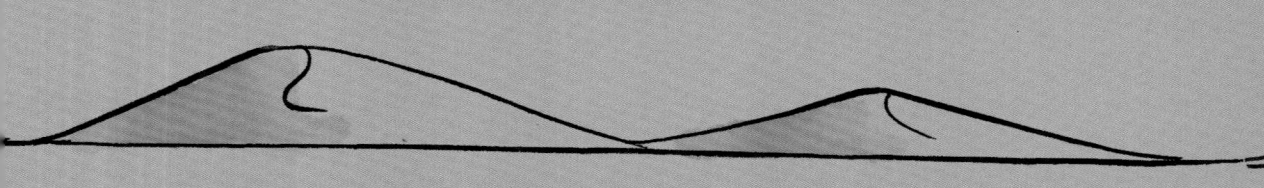

Twirling around, Ostrich halted mid-spin when she saw the dazzling figure.

"Honey, aren't you a sight for sore eyes?" Then she sighed. "The world used to be filled with beautiful colors. I don't know what happened."

"I think the color switch got turned off. I'm trying to find it and flip it on," Guion explained.

Brightening, Ostrich remarked, "Sugar, that's a marvelous idea! Good luck! And thanks for rescuing me."

Guion waved goodbye, continuing on his quest, until a fast-moving ball bowled him right over.

Skidding to a stop, Pangolin uncurled his body, saw the radiant roadblock sprawled before him and promptly tucked his head.

"What's your hurry?" Guion asked, dusting himself off.

Without peeking, Pangolin muttered, "I'm late. I'm rolling to the river as fast as I can."

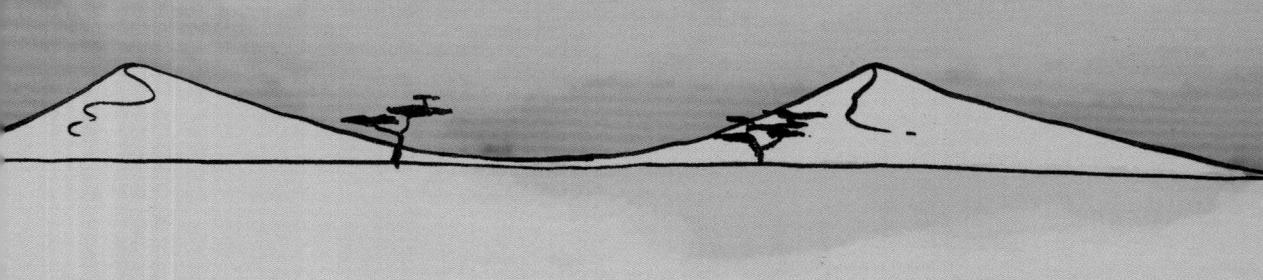

"I'm lightning quick – jump on!" Guion offered.

Pangolin shook his head. "No, thanks, Mr. Lion. I learned very early to take care of myself."

"Even if I can help?" asked Guion.

Finally, Pangolin looked into the lion's kind eyes. "I am in a big rush," he whispered and awkwardly climbed on.

As they traveled, Guion inquired, "Any idea where I might find the switch to turn on the missing colors?"

Pangolin shrugged. "No, but I've heard stories of brighter places."

Arriving at the river, Pangolin rolled off and said, "Thanks for the ride. You were a big help after all."

With the setting sun, Guion encountered a frantic monkey pacing the river's edge.

"What's got you in a tizzy?" the inquisitive lion asked.

"See those delicious berries? I'm starving, but I can't swim!" he complained.

"Hop on! I'll paddle you across," Guion offered.

Looking the strange lion up and down, Monkey grumbled, "You're so different."

"Suit yourself, but it's no bother," Guion answered cheerfully.

Monkey inspected him again. "Well, I am really hungry."

"Wow!" Monkey shrieked, seeing Guion's colorful reflection on the water.

When they reached the other side of the river, Monkey jumped off, yelling behind him, "Thanks for the swim and the color show!"

Panting, Guion called out, "Have you seen the switch...?"

But the frenzied Monkey had already scurried up the tree.

Tired from his adventures, Guion settled into the tall grass and surveyed the dim world around him.

"This place feels so lonely," he sighed, "but I know color will change everything. I'll try again in the morning."

As dawn was breaking, Guion awakened to something he hadn't heard in a while - laughter.

Hurrying toward the sound, he discovered the animals mingling together in a rainbow of beautiful colors.

When they saw Guion, they raced to him, chattering in excited voices.

"Elephant couldn't reach the fruit, so I handed him one. Suddenly, green spilled over his trunk and danced up my arm!" screeched Monkey.

Ostrich called, "Ooh, ooh! When Cheetah agreed to let me deliver his message, swirls of orange burst across my gorgeous feathers and his spotted fur. Sugar, it was amazing!"

"Mr. Lion," Pangolin squeaked. "I did it, too! I rolled across Hippo's back to scratch an itch she couldn't reach. Next thing we knew, purple stripes covered us both!"

Guion beamed. "Spectacular! You found the switch!"

"We all did!" cheered the animals.

As he watched the bright yellow sun rise against a glowing pink and blue sky, Guion smiled.

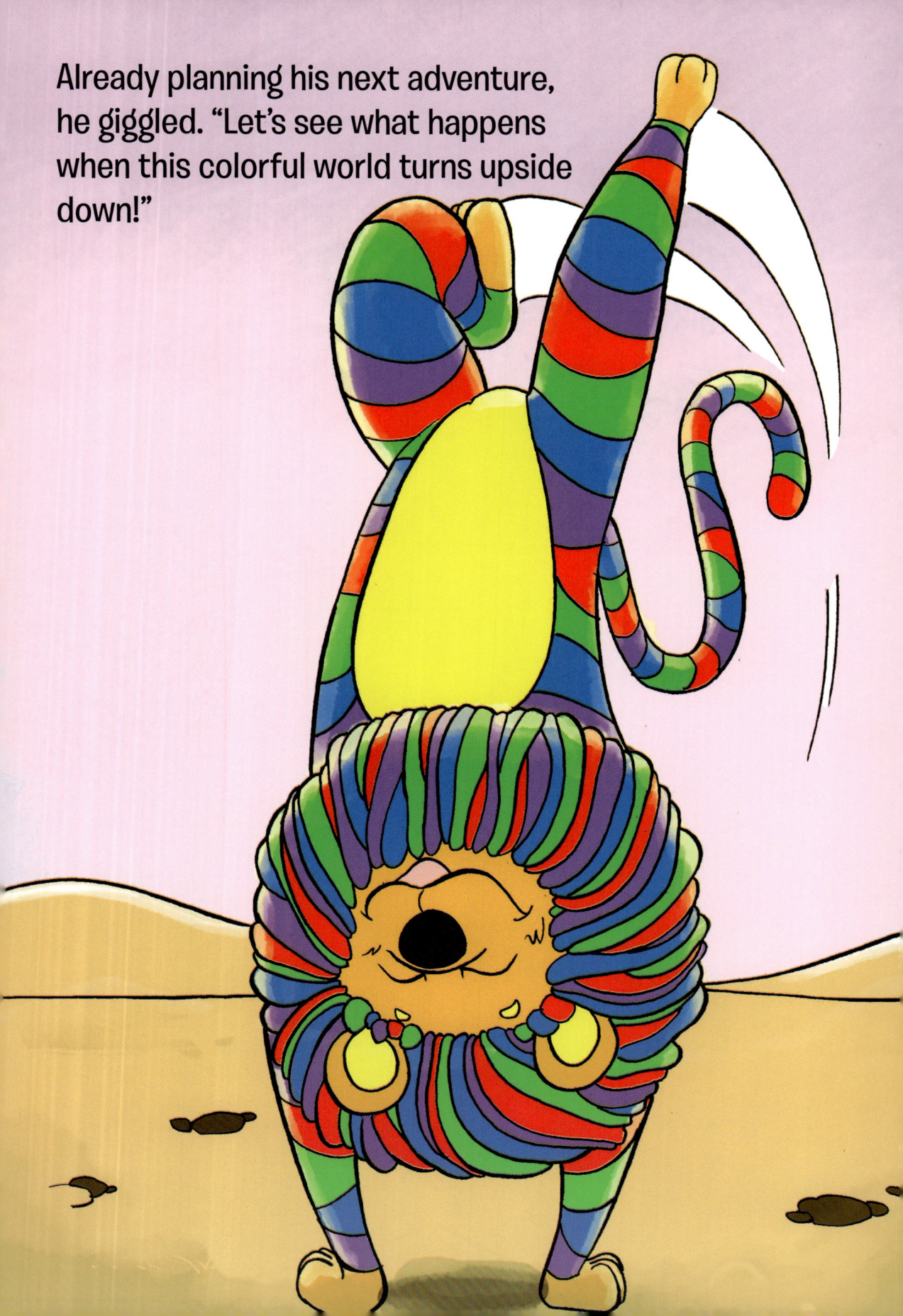

Already planning his next adventure, he giggled. "Let's see what happens when this colorful world turns upside down!"